DATE DUE

MAY 4 - 2006	JUL 3 0 2007
	NOV 3 0 2007
	DEC 1 3 2007
AUG 2 8 2006	FEB 1 6 2008
OCT 1 0 2006	
MAR 3 1 2007	
APR 2 3 200	

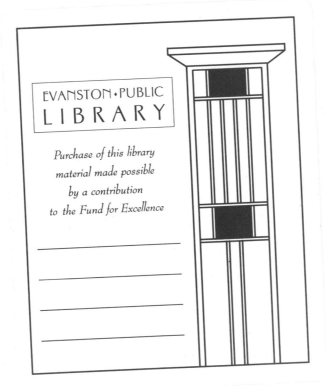

Phonics Friends

Akiko, Miss Alice, and the Dance Class
The Sound of Short A

The
**Child's
World**

By Cecilia Minden and Joanne Meier

Published in the United States of America
by The Child's World®
PO Box 326
Chanhassen, MN 55317-0326
800-599-READ
www.childsworld.com

A special thank you to Ann Kurokawa and the students
of the "Picture Us Different" dance studio in Park Ridge,
Illinois, for allowing us to photograph their talents.

The Child's World®: Mary Berendes, Publishing Director

Editorial Directions, Inc.: E. Russell Primm, Editorial
Director and Project Editor; Katie Marsico, Associate
Editor; Judith Shiffer, Associate Editor and School Media
Specialist; Linda S. Koutris, Photo Researcher and
Selector

The Design Lab: Kathleen Petelinsek, Design and Page
Production

Photographs ©: Photo setting and photography by Romie
and Alice Flanagan/Flanagan Publishing Services

Library of Congress Cataloging-in-Publication Data
Minden, Cecilia.
  Akiko, Miss Alice, and the dance class : the sound of
short A / by Cecilia Minden and Joanne Meier.
     p. cm. — (Phonics friends)
  Summary: Simple text, featuring the short A, describes
Akiko's tap dance class with Miss Alice.
  ISBN 1-59296-312-9 (library bound : alk. paper)
[1. English language—Phonetics. 2. Reading.] I. Meier,
Joanne D. II. Title. III. Series.
  PZ7.M6539Ak 2004
  [E]—dc22   2004001973

Note to parents and educators:

The Child's World® has created Phonics Friends with the goal of exposing children to engaging stories and pictures that assist in phonics development. The books in the series will help children learn the relationships between the letters of written language and the individual sounds of spoken language. This contact helps children learn to use these relationships to read and write words.

The books in this series follow a similar format. An introductory page, to be read by an adult, introduces the child to the phonics feature, or sound, that will be highlighted in the book. Read this page to the child, stressing the phonic feature. Help the student learn how to form the sound with her mouth. The Phonics Friends story and engaging photographs follow the introduction. At the end of the story, word lists categorize the feature words into their phonic element. Additional information on using these lists is on The Child's World® Web site listed at the top of this page.

Each book in this series has been carefully written to meet specific readability requirements. Close attention has been paid to elements such as word count, sentence length, and vocabulary. Readability formulas measure the ease with which the text can be read and understood. Each Phonics Friends book has been analyzed using the Spache readability formula. For more information on this formula, as well as the levels for each of the books in this series please visit The Child's World® Web site.

Reading research suggests that systematic phonics instruction can greatly improve students' word recognition, spelling, and comprehension skills. The Phonics Friends series assists in the teaching of phonics by providing students with important opportunities to apply their knowledge of phonics as they read words, sentences, and text.

The letter *a* makes two sounds.

The long sound of *a* sounds like *a* as in:

    cake and *date*.

The short sound of *a* sounds like *a* as in:

    cat and *add*.

In this book, you will read words that
have the short *a* sound as in:

    dance, bag, apple, and *tap*.

Akiko likes to dance.

Her shoes are in her bag.

Akiko has an apple in her bag.

The apple is for her teacher,

Miss Alice.

Akiko gives Miss Alice the apple.

"Thank you, Akiko," says

Miss Alice.

Akiko puts on her tap shoes.

She gets in the line.

Miss Alice claps her hands.

The music begins.

Miss Alice taps her foot.

Akiko taps her foot.

The girls clap and tap.

They tap around the room.

Akiko likes to hear her

tapping toes!

I love to dance!

It makes me happy.

Fun Facts

Not all apples are red—some are green or yellow, too. There are 7,500 different types of apples grown all over the world. Some apple trees can live for more than 100 years! The states that produce the most apples are Washington, New York, Michigan, California, Pennsylvania, and Virginia. In Michigan, the blossom found on apple trees is the state flower.

Tap dancing is a combination of English, Scottish, Irish, and African cultures. Metal is attached to the heels and toes of tap shoes. This is what makes the tapping noise when dancers perform. Before metal was used, some tap dancers used shoes made of wood. Tap dancing became popular in the United States in the late 1800s.

Activity

Apple Picking
If you like apples, then you should consider going apple picking with your family. Certain farms and orchards allow people to collect apples and then take them home. Apple picking usually begins in the fall. When you get home, you and your parents can bake an apple pie for the whole family to enjoy!

To Learn More

Books
About the Sound of Short A
Flanagan, Alice K. *Cats: The Sound of Short A*. Chanhassen, Minn.: The Child's World, 2000.
Chapman, Joan. *An Ant: Learning the Short A Sound*. New York: Powerkids Press, 2002.

About Apples
Klingel, Cynthia, and Robert B. Noyed. *Apples*. Chanhassen, Minn.: The Child's World, 2001.
Maestro, Betsy, and Giulio Maestro. *How Do Apples Grow?* New York: HarperCollins, 1992.

About Clapping Hands
Bernstein, Sara. *Hand Clap! "Miss Mary Mack" and 42 Other Handclapping Games for Children*. Holbrook, Mass.: Adams Media Corporation, 1994.

About Tap Dancing
Thomas, Mark. *Tap Dancing*. Danbury, Conn.: Children's Press, 2001.
Paraskevas, Betty, and Michael Paraskevas. *Marvin the Tap-Dancing Horse*. New York: Simon & Schuster Books for Young Readers, 2001.

Web Sites
Visit our home page for lots of links about the Sound of Short A:
http://www.childsworld.com/links.html

Note to Parents, Teachers, and Librarians: We routinely check our Web links to make sure they're safe, active sites—so encourage your readers to check them out!

Short A Feature Words

Proper Names
Akiko

Alice

Feature Word in Initial Position
apple

Feature Words in Medial Position
bag

clap

dance

hand

happy

tap

tapping

About the Authors

Cecilia Minden, PhD, directs the Language and Literacy Program at the Harvard Graduate School of Education. She is a reading specialist with classroom and administrative experience in grades K–12. She earned her PhD in reading education from the University of Virginia. Cecilia and her husband Dave Cupp enjoy sharing their love of reading with their granddaughter Chelsea.

Joanne Meier, PhD, has worked as an elementary school teacher and university professor. She earned her BA in early childhood education from the University of South Carolina, and her MEd and PhD in education from the University of Virginia. She currently works as a literacy consultant for schools and private organizations. Joanne Meier lives with her husband Eric, and spends most of her time chasing her two daughters, Kella and Erin, and her two cats, Sam and Gilly, in Charlottesville, Virginia.